2.2

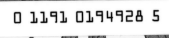

HELLO MUDDAH, HELLO FADDAH!
(A LETTER FROM CAMP)

by **Allan Sherman** and **Lou Busch**
illustrated by **Jack E. Davis**

PUFFIN BOOKS

For Lucy, Janey, and Vincent
J.E.D.

PUFFIN BOOKS
Published by the Penguin Group
Penguin Young Readers Group, 345 Hudson Street,
New York, New York 10014, U.S.A.

Registered Offices: Penguin Books Ltd, 80 Strand, London WC2R 0RL, England

First published in the United States of America by Dutton Children's Books,
a division of Penguin Young Readers Group, 2004
Published by Puffin Books, a division of Penguin Young Readers Group, 2006

1 3 5 7 9 10 8 6 4 2

Words by Allan Sherman
Music by Lou Busch
Copyright © WB Music Corp. and Burning Bush Music, 1963 (Renewed 1991)
Illustrations copyright © Jack E. Davis, 2004
CIP Data is available.

Puffin Books ISBN 0-14-240638-4
Printed in the United States of America

Camp is very entertaining,

and they say we'll have some
fun if it stops raining.

I went hiking with Joe Spivy.

He developed poison ivy.

All the counselors
hate the waiters,

and the lake has alligators,

and the head coach
wants no sissies,
so he reads to us from
something called *Ulysses*.

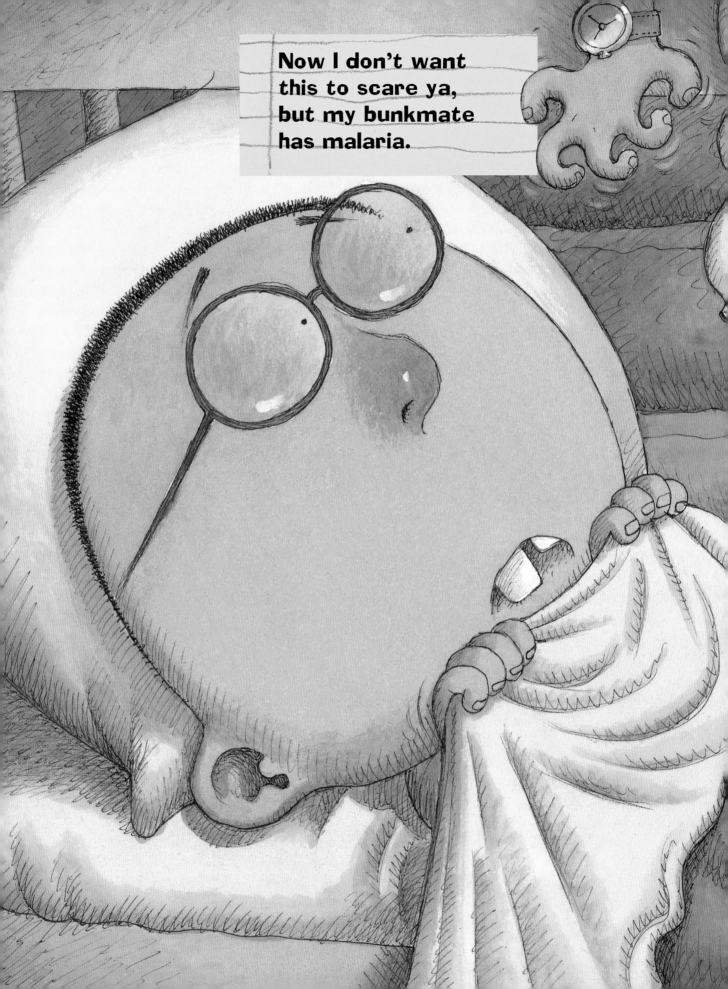

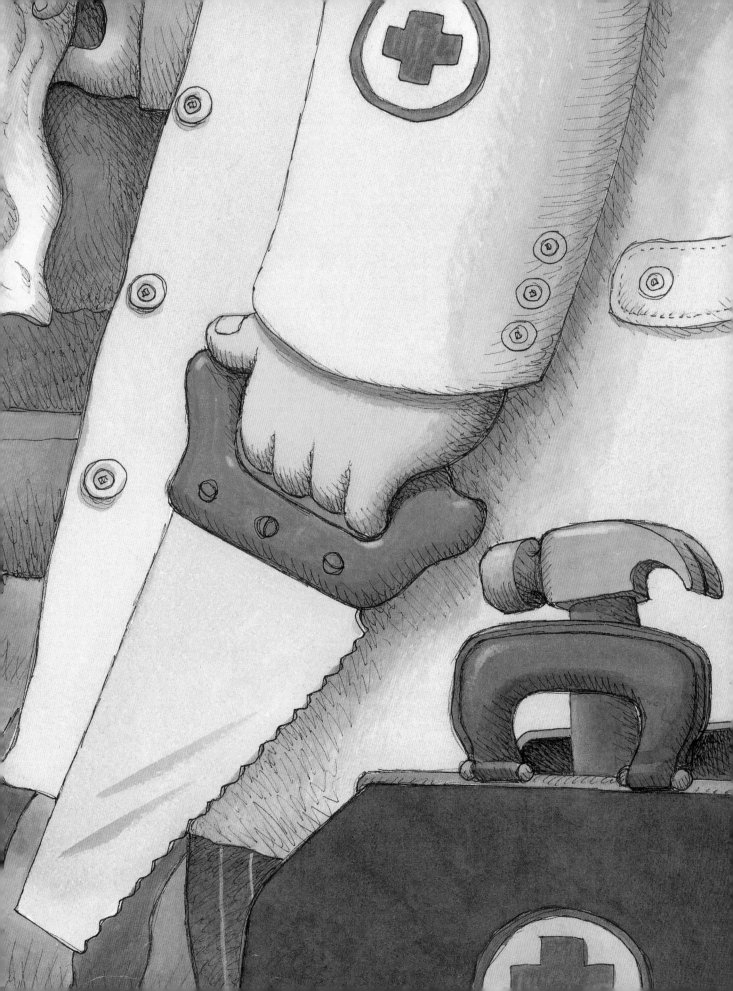

Take me home, oh Muddah, Faddah, take me home. I hate Granada.

Don't leave me out in the forest where I might get eaten by a bear.

Take me home, I promise
I will not make noise
or mess the house with other boys.

Dearest Faddah, darling Muddah,
how's my precious little bruddah?

Let me come home if you miss me.
I would even let Aunt Bertha hug and
kiss me.

**Playing baseball,
gee that's better.**

Muddah, Faddah, kindly disregard this letter.